SPACE
PIRATES

AND OTHER SCI-FI STORIES

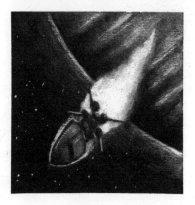

T700032518920

Illustr

A & C Black • London

'Alien Invasion!' will help less confident readers gain more independence
'This is Not Earth' and 'Space Pirates' are for independent readers
'Everything I Need' is for experienced readers

First published 2008 by
A & C Black Publishers Ltd
38 Soho Square, London, W1D 3HB

www.acblack.com

Text copyright © 2008 Tony Bradman
Illustrations copyright © 2008 Mark Oldroyd

ISBN 978-0-7136-8905-1

A CIP catalogue for this book is available from the British Library.

CONTENTS

ALIEN INVASION!

6

"What on *earth* is wrong with your hamster, Megan?" said Dad in a cross voice. "This is the third night running that he's woken me up."

Megan slowly opened her eyes and stared at the strange creature in her bedroom doorway. It had wild hair, a grumpy face, and a big picture of Darth Vader on its chest. For a second, Megan wondered if she was still asleep and having a terrible dream. Then she realised the creature was actually her dad, and that he was in his pyjamas. He had been a *Star Wars* fan ever since he was little.

But Dad was *not* a fan of Harry, Megan's pet hamster.

"Sorry, Dad," said Megan. She quickly got out of bed and crossed the dark room. Harry's cage was under her desk, and she could hear him thundering round on his squeaky exercise wheel.

"I just don't get it," Dad muttered, glaring at Harry as Megan reached into the cage and picked up her pet. "He shouldn't be leaping around at his age, he should be slowing down, taking it easy. For a hamster he's practically an old-age pensioner. You must have had him for years now."

"Since my sixth birthday," said Megan, rubbing her cheek against Harry's warm, furry head, cross that Dad didn't remember. Harry was five now, and Dad was right, he *was* old for a hamster. So it was rather odd that he seemed to have got loads of energy from somewhere. He had been tearing round the exercise wheel like a mad thing, and Megan could feel his heart hammering away inside his little body.

"Well, he'd better start being a bit calmer, or he'll find himself spending his nights in the garden shed," said Dad. "I've had enough."

"But… you can't do that!" squealed Megan, hugging Harry to her chest. "It's cruelty to animals. He'll die out there in the cold!"

"What about cruelty to fathers?" said Dad. "I need my beauty sleep."

"You can say that again…" Megan muttered under her breath.

"Very funny," said Dad. "Now I suggest you put Mr Frantic back in his cage and get into bed yourself. We'll talk in the morning."

Things were rather hectic the next day, though. Mum and Dad had woken up late, and Dad was doing a lot of complaining about it all being a certain mad hamster's fault. Mum, however, was too busy trying to tear Megan's brother Lewis away from the TV to listen.

"Read my lips, Lewis," said Mum. "I'm going to start counting, and if you aren't upstairs cleaning your teeth by the time I reach five, you'll be banned from watching TV for the rest of your life. One… two… three…"

"OK, OK…" grumbled Lewis. "But I was only watching the news. Did you know that scientists in America have detected a giant cloud of meteorites heading towards Earth?"

"I bet they couldn't detect any brains inside your head, though," said Megan. "They'd need the biggest telescope in the world to do that."

Lewis stuck out his tongue, and his sister did the same. Soon the two of them were yelling at each other, and Mum joined in.

"Ah, family life, don't you just love it?" said Dad. "Maybe if I'm lucky I'll get struck by one of those meteorites and put out of my misery."

Ten minutes later, they were in the car, heading into the nearby town to school and work.

Megan worried about Harry all day, and checked on him as soon as she got home that afternoon. He was quiet and dozy now, but she spent most of the evening in her room, keeping an eye on him.

Eventually, Mum told her to get into bed, and soon Megan was fast asleep. But she didn't stay that way for long. She was woken by a noise, though this time Harry wasn't to blame. Megan sat up in bed, listening to the deep, throbbing sound. Harry was standing on his hind legs, hanging on to the bars of his cage, innocently staring up at her.

She heard her parents' bedroom door open, and footsteps cross the landing.

"I *don't* believe it," Dad muttered, coming into Megan's room. "What's your hamster doing now? It sounds like he's *driving* round his exercise wheel in a racing car!"

"It's nothing to do with Harry," said Megan. She got out of bed and went over to check on her pet. "I mean, it's *obviously* coming from outside."

The noise seemed to deepen and grow in volume, and bright light suddenly burst in round the edges of the blind.

"What the *heck* is going on out there?" Dad said. He lifted the blind to look outside, but immediately backed off, dazzled by the light, and stomped downstairs. Megan slipped out on to the landing and saw Mum heading downstairs, too. Lewis was in the doorway to his room, his hair sticking up. Brother and sister exchanged a look, and Megan shrugged.

"Back to bed, you two," said Mum.

"You must be joking," said Lewis, and hurried after her, a big grin on his face. "Come on, sis, don't you want to know what's happening?"

"I suppose so," said Megan and started to follow him. But then she paused, and went back to pick up Harry's cage. She covered it with the cloth they used when they took him to the vet, so he wouldn't get frightened. Later, when she thought about it, she didn't understand why she'd done it. But she was very glad she had…

By the time Megan got downstairs, the rest of her family had gone into the garden. She could see the three of them standing there, looking upwards, bathed in a dazzling, eerie light that was coming from directly above. The throbbing noise had grown so intense, Megan could feel it in every part of her body. There was no movement in Harry's cage, though, and Megan hoped he was OK.

She joined her parents and brother in the garden, and looked up as well – then she drew her breath in sharply. An enormous, gleaming object was descending slowly towards them. It was metallic silver, perfectly circular and smooth, and was the source of both the throbbing noise and the light.

"Oh… wow!" she said, awestruck. "Er… is that what I think it is?"

"I hope so," murmured Lewis. "I'll be pretty disappointed if it isn't."

"You don't seriously believe that's a flying saucer, do you?" said Mum.

"What else could it be?" said Dad, his voice shaking with excitement. "We're about to have a close encounter, right here in the back garden."

"The shed is going to have a much closer one," said Lewis.

The flying saucer finally landed in the garden, crushing the garden shed beneath it. Dad groaned, but Megan couldn't help feeling pleased. He wouldn't be able to put Harry in there now.

"Whoops!" said Mum. "They park just like you, dear."

Megan and Lewis sniggered, and Dad opened his mouth to reply, but a sudden hissing noise came from the saucer and made them jump. Mum squeaked, grabbed hold of both children and dragged them behind her husband.

"Look, there's a hatch!" said Lewis, pointing. "And it's opening…"

Megan peered at the saucer and saw that he was right. A section of the saucer's surface had slid open, revealing a dark hole with wisps of steam rising from it. Then there was a loud humming, and a ramp poked out like a long, metal tongue. Its tip came to rest on the grass.

"I don't like it," Mum whispered. "What if they're not friendly?"

"I'm sure they will be, if we are," said Dad. "Smile, everybody."

Megan and Lewis exchanged another look and rolled their eyes. But they did as they were told, and Mum tried to smile, too. But their expressions soon changed when the occupants of the saucer appeared.

Five dark figures marched down the ramp, their boots clanging on the metal. They advanced up the garden towards the huddle of humans. Megan thought at first they might be human, too. But as they got closer, she began to see just how alien they were.

They each appeared to have two arms, two legs and one head. They were much taller than most human beings, though, and their faces were simply terrifying – all slimy white skin, staring yellow eyes and cruel red mouths. Their powerful bodies were covered in what looked like uniforms, and each alien was wearing the same close-fitting black outfit. They were carrying short tubes that could only be guns.

The aliens stopped in front of them, one standing ahead of the others. He was slightly taller, and Megan assumed he was the leader.

"Surrender, Earthlings," he said in a harsh voice. "We are the Krell, and this planet is now ours. If you resist you will be... *utterly destroyed!*"

"Hey, steady on," said Dad. "There's no need to be so aggressive. You can't go around taking other people's planets and threatening them."

"Quite right," said Mum. "Apart from anything else, it's very rude."

"*SILENCE!*" roared the alien. "You will obey us or you will die. The rest of our fleet is in orbit round the planet and will be landing soon."

"Hey, I bet that's the cloud of meteorites I heard about on the news," said Lewis. "What a great disguise for an invasion fleet. This is so cool!"

"That's not how I'd describe it," muttered Dad. "Now listen, Mr Alien, whatever your name is, I think you just need to calm down…"

"Our patience is gone," hissed the alien leader. "Prepare to die!"

Then several things happened at once. The aliens raised their weapons and pointed them at the humans. Dad yelled "No!", and Mum screamed, pulling Megan and Lewis even closer to her. That jogged Megan's arm, which made Harry's cage tilt to one side and the cloth slip off, revealing the hamster, who started squeaking loudly.

The instant the aliens saw Harry, they gasped. They lowered their weapons and threw themselves on the grass with outstretched arms.

17

"All hail, Oh Mighty Beast!" the alien leader moaned. "Forgive us! We had no idea that you had already taken this planet as your own..."

Mum, Dad and Lewis were looking stunned, but Megan's mind was racing. For some reason, the aliens seemed frightened of Harry!

"Er... excuse me, Mr Alien..." said Megan. "Do you have creatures like this where you come from?"

"Oh yes," said the alien leader. "We worship them as gods."

"Really?" said Megan, smiling. "Well, the Great God Harry the Hamster has something to say. Listen, and I'll tell you what it is..."

"What are you doing?" Dad hissed out of the corner of his mouth.

Megan ignored him. She leaned down and pretended to listen to her hamster. "What's that, Harry?" she said. Harry gave a little squeak. It was almost as if he was joining in with the deception. "You're ordering the Krell to leave Earth immediately, or you'll have them destroyed – this is your planet now. Did you hear that, Mr Alien? You've made the Great God *very* angry."

"We hear you," said the alien leader. Megan could see that he was shaking with fear. "And we shall obey... instantly."

They walked backwards into their flying saucer, bowing and scraping all the way, and soon the spaceship was rising slowly, throbbing and flashing with light as it had done on its descent.

Megan felt hugely relieved. But then the spaceship paused and seemed to be hovering over the garden. "Uh oh, maybe they've changed their minds..." she murmured.

Suddenly a beam of dazzling, silver light shot down on to the spot where the spaceship had landed. There was a crackling noise, the light went out – and when they looked, they saw that the shed been completely restored.

"*SORRY!*" A harsh voice boomed out. Then the saucer shot up into the sky at enormous speed and disappeared.

"Well done, sweetheart," said Mum, giving Megan a big hug.

"Yeah, that was pretty cool, sis," said Lewis. "You saved the world!"

"Actually, it was Harry who did that," said Megan, and Harry squeaked in his cage. "So he probably deserves some thanks – don't you agree, Dad?"

"Fine," said Dad, and shrugged. "But I'm not treating him like a god."

"You don't have to," said Megan. "I'm sure he'll be happy just as things are... so long as you promise not to make him spend his nights in the shed."

"OK," said Dad with a sigh. "I'll just have to get some earplugs."

And that, thought Megan, seemed like a very good plan indeed.

THIS IS NOT EARTH

Jamie was skimming along a dried-up river bed on his hover-bike when his helmet radio buzzed for the third time. He tried to ignore it and concentrate on the sheer joy of the ride, the cool wind in his face, the planet's pink sky above, the purple sand sweeping past beneath him.

But the buzzing wouldn't go away. It kept on and on, like the irritating whine of an insect trapped inside his ear. Eventually, Jamie could stand it no more, and slowed the hover-bike to a stop. He had known all along that he couldn't avoid speaking to his parents.

"Hey, Dad," he said. He didn't have to touch anything on the helmet – the reply function was voice activated. "Er... what can I do for you?"

"Well, you could answer your radio for a start," said his father. "This is the third time we've tried to call you. We were beginning to get worried."

"Sorry," said Jamie. "I should have

realised you'd want to stop me having *fun*. It's probably bad for me to be out *in the open air*."

Jamie had always been close to his mum and dad, and wouldn't usually have talked to them like that, but a few weeks ago he had guessed what they were planning, and he'd been angry with them ever since. So there had been a lot of arguments. Today, however, it seemed that Dad had no intention of reacting to his son's tone of voice.

"Just come home, Jamie," he said with a sigh. "We need to talk."

"I can't *wait*," muttered Jamie, and angrily broke the connection. He boosted the power on the hover-bike once more, rose out of the river bed, and grimly headed back towards his parents' farm.

The surface of the planet stretched before him – a dusty, purple plain ringed by hills, with colossal, white-capped mountains rising beyond. It was an alien world, slightly smaller than Earth and orbiting a distant star, a red giant. But Jamie didn't think of it as alien, for he had never lived in humanity's original home. Of course he had seen films of Earth, and pictures of the beautiful place it had been before endless wars and pollution finally ruined it for human life.

The survivors had abandoned the wrecked cities and dying lands and poisoned oceans, and taken off in a fleet of starships to find somewhere else to live. Jamie's parents had met on the *Galileo* in the first few months after The Great Exodus, as it was now called. And that's where Jamie had been born, 12 Earth-years ago – in deep space.

Until a while back, all he had known was life on a starship. If you could call it life. Jamie scowled as he remembered the *Galileo*. Dozens of families packed into a filthy tin can, the air stale, the food produced by machines and almost inedible, disputes always breaking out because nobody had any privacy. Then there was the sickness the doctors couldn't cure, however hard they tried. Space Fever killed many, and left the lucky ones – like Jamie – with nasty sores to remember it by. The sores were often raw and painful, and seemed permanent. Jamie and his parents had hoped that living on a planet might help, but it hadn't.

Jamie reached the crest of a hill and let the hover-bike slow to a stop again. He sat there for a moment looking down on the farm, a cluster of silver domes in a small valley. He scratched the weeping sore on his hand and thought of the day when he and his parents had landed. He'd been happy enough when he'd found out they'd been given the chance to colonise a planet, even one that didn't have a name, only a code number, K1754. But he'd never imagined just how incredible it would be.

The clean, crisp freshness of the air, the sense of wide-open spaces and total freedom – Jamie loved the place from the moment he stepped out of the shuttle craft that had brought them down from the starship.

In the year since then, Jamie had spent as much time as he could roaming on the hover-bike his dad had built for him. The planet was mostly desert, with scant rainfall and few plants. There weren't many animals either, apart from a squirrel-like rodent, some tiny reptiles, and strange flying creatures that resembled large bats. Even so, the more Jamie got to know this world, the more it felt like the home he had always wanted. But his parents didn't feel the same, and that was the problem.

Jamie's helmet radio buzzed once more. "OK, OK," he sighed, zooming off down the hill. "I'm on my way…"

As he skimmed along, Jamie tried not to look at the fields his parents had planted using frozen seeds from the *Galileo*'s gene banks – the wheat struggling to survive, the stunted vegetables, the dead fruit-tree saplings. Jamie stopped by the entrance to the largest dome, the family's living quarters. He got off his hover-bike and removed his helmet, took a deep breath, touched the panel that opened the door... and went inside.

As usual, his parents were busy. Dad was in the kitchen area preparing the evening meal, Mum was working on the computer, probably checking their stores. There wasn't much space inside, but it was like a palace compared to the tiny cabin they'd had back on the *Galileo*. The dome was divided into three, the kitchen/living room and two sleeping areas, so Jamie even had his own bedroom.

"Dinner will be in ten minutes," said Dad, glancing at him and smiling nervously. "It's your favourite... chicken stew with vegetables."

Jamie shrugged. Dad's stew wasn't bad, but it wasn't that great, either. The chicken wasn't real, of course, but some kind of substitute made on the *Galileo*. They'd brought a lot of food with them, which was just as well. But they were still a long way from being self-sufficient.

"And then after dinner we're going to watch a movie," said Mum, smiling, too. "It's time we did something nice together, as a family."

"What, instead of arguing?" muttered Jamie. "I thought Dad said we needed to talk. I know what you're going to say anyway, so let's get it over with."

"Don't be like that, Jamie," said Mum. She came over to put an arm around him, but he pulled away. "We're only thinking of you…"

"Oh, yeah?" said Jamie. "That's not how it feels to me. I want to stay here, but you don't. We're going back to the *Galileo*, aren't we?"

Jamie's parents looked at each other, their smiles gone now.

"We don't really have much choice," Dad said quietly, his shoulders sagging as if he were very, very tired. "You know how hard your mum and I have tried, but we just can't make the farm work. None of the crops we've planted are thriving."

"Maybe they need more time," said Jamie.

"You're not giving them a proper chance. They're Earth plants and, if you haven't noticed, this is not Earth. They might do OK in a couple of years…"

"You may be right," said Mum. "But I'm afraid we don't have time to wait. The truth is we're going to run out of food in a couple of *weeks*, and the captain of the *Galileo* won't give us supplies after that. Not unless we can give him something in return."

"And that's not likely to happen, is it?" said Dad. He started ladling the stew into bowls, then paused to smile at his son again. "Come on, Jamie, don't be cross. We'll only be on the *Galileo* a while, until they find another planet for us. A few months won't be so bad, will it?"

"But I like *this* planet," Jamie yelled. "I don't want to try anywhere else. And what if they don't find one we can settle on? You told me there aren't many planets with an atmosphere people can breathe, or where it's not too hot or too cold. We might be stuck on the *Galileo* for ever!"

"We don't want that any more than you do," said Mum. "We'd love to stay here. We'd give anything to make it possible. But we can't. So that's it, end of story. I'm sorry, Jamie. The shuttle is coming to collect us… tomorrow."

Jamie felt as if all the blood had suddenly drained out of his body. His parents were looking at him, obviously waiting for him to speak, to argue with them. He opened his mouth to do just that, but what could he say that hadn't already been said? So he closed it, then turned on his heel and went into his bedroom, slamming the flimsy plastic door behind him.

Jamie stayed in his room all evening, refusing to come out and watch the movie or speak to his parents. Dad brought him a bowl of stew, which he left untouched, and Mum tried to talk to him. But Jamie was playing a computer game and wouldn't look at her. He was more angry than ever, and he wanted them to know it.

When they put their heads round the door to say goodnight, Jamie ignored them, although he did get into bed. Then he lay there, unable to sleep, scratching at his sores and remembering all the things he hated about the *Galileo* – the overcrowding, the people suffering from Space Fever... He felt sick just thinking that the next time he went to bed it would be in a cramped little cabin, with Mum and Dad squeezed in beside him.

Suddenly Jamie knew he would much rather stay on the planet and die than get on the shuttle tomorrow and fly back into space. So why didn't he do just that? He could simply run away and hide. He knew the place much better than Mum and Dad – they would never find him. A few last days of freedom would be worth more than a whole lifetime on board the *Galileo*. He sat up and quickly started to put on his clothes. Not that he really wanted to die, of course...

Jamie carefully slipped from his bedroom and crept over to the kitchen area. He put a handful of energy snacks in his backpack, added a big bottle of water from the fridge, then made for the main door. He was pretty sure Mum and Dad wouldn't hear him. Dad said they were usually so tired they slept like the dead. Even so, Jamie's heart was hammering hard as he touched the panel and the door hissed open.

Outside, the planet's three small moons were shining, so there was plenty of light to see by. Jamie pulled on his helmet and climbed on to the hover-bike. Soon he was heading away from the farm, back up into the hills, grateful that the hover-bike's motor was almost silent. With a bit of luck, Mum and Dad wouldn't discover he was gone until the morning.

Jamie skimmed along, an eerie, triple shadow gliding over the dark sand beside him. The wind was colder than it had been earlier, and he knew the temperature would drop even further during the night. He was wearing his thick, outdoors jacket, so he should be OK. But it would still be good to spend a few hours under shelter if he could, and maybe get some sleep. He knew just the right place, too – a valley with a small pond and a cave on the slope nearby.

By the time he reached the mouth of the cave, two of the moons had gone down, and most of the valley was in darkness. The place was the same as ever, although Jamie noticed there were some new, tall plants around the pond. He couldn't see them clearly, but was too tired to look at them closely right now. Moments later, after checking the cave was empty, Jamie settled in for the night.

He slept on the sand just inside the cave, wrapped in his jacket, head on his backpack. It was a restless, dream-filled sleep, and he was glad to be woken by the warm rays of the sun touching his face. Jamie stood and stretched, his body stiff and aching. He opened his backpack, took out an energy snack and drank some water. He wondered if Mum and Dad had discovered that he'd run away.

As if on cue, his helmet radio started buzzing. It was sitting on the seat of his hover-bike, where he'd left it last night. Jamie went over to pick it up, tempted to answer. He was beginning to feel he'd done something stupid, and that it was wrong to worry Mum and Dad.

Then he saw the plants by the pond in the clear light of day. There was something rather strange about them so, ignoring the buzzing noise, he went down the slope for a closer look.

The plants had thick, tall stems, and were clustered along one edge of the pond, where they could get most sunlight. But it was their leaves that had caught Jamie's attention. They were dark red and grew directly out of the stems in pairs, one on either side, perhaps 20 pairs to a plant. Jamie reached out to touch a leaf and, as he did so, the tip of another one brushed against the sore on his hand. The skin around it instantly began to tingle, and he snatched it back. Then the tingling became intense...

Jamie watched in amazement as the sore on his hand vanished. He rubbed at the skin, but where it had once been raw and painful, it was now healed. Jamie broke off a different leaf from a second plant and cautiously rubbed it over a sore on his arm. Exactly the same thing happened. It was incredible – and then Jamie realised how important this discovery could be. The planet itself, good old K1754, might just have given him the solution to his problem. Maybe this was a cure for Space Fever…

He ran back up the slope, picked up his helmet, and quickly put it on. "Jamie calling Mum and Dad," he gabbled. "Can you hear me?"

"Jamie!" said his dad. "Where are you? We've been so worried."

"Listen, Dad," said Jamie. "You said we'd only be able to stay here if we had something we could give the captain of the *Galileo* in return for more supplies. Well, you're not going to believe what I've found…"

"What are you talking about?" said Dad. "Are you sure you're OK?"

"Relax, Dad, I'm fine," said Jamie. He looked down at the red leaf in his hand. "In fact, I've never felt better. I'll see you and Mum in a while."

Moments later, Jamie was skimming along on his hover-bike once more, the cool wind in his face, the pink sky above and purple sand beneath him. His pockets were stuffed with red leaves, and he was smiling. And this time it felt good to be going home.

SPACE PIRATES

Kyle Raker stood in the hatch of the spaceship *Happy Rakers* and looked across Rigel 3's landing site. The sandy ground was crowded with other spacecraft, and beings from everywhere in the galaxy bustled between them and the silver domes of the port. But there was still no sign of Dad.

"Where *is* he, Gizmo?" Kyle said to the robodog beside him. Gizmo bleeped, his plastic ears drooping. Kyle glanced at the yellow sky and the twin red suns setting over the mountains. The *Happy Rakers* was resting horizontally on its tripod of landing legs, a double shadow stretching behind it. "We should have left this planet ages ago. Dad *promised*…"

Kyle sighed, turned, and trudged back through the ship, his spaceboots clanging on the metal deck. It wasn't a long walk – the *Happy Rakers* was only a C-class freighter, a medium-sized vessel with a cargo hold, plus some basic living quarters. The bridge was a large area in the spaceship's bows, dominated by a big viewing screen, with other, smaller screens and dials filling the curved side walls.

Kyle sat down in the co-pilot's seat, and Gizmo sprung on to his lap. Soon, Kyle was brooding about just how awful his life was.

Dad was a trader and travelled round the galaxy, buying and selling anything to make a profit. A few months back, Dad had promised Kyle and his mum a trip to World of Fun, the coolest theme-park planet in 500 star systems. But lately business had been terrible, and Dad had suddenly announced they couldn't afford a holiday after all.

Kyle had been so disappointed that Mum had suggested Dad bring him along on this day trip instead. It was obvious Mum had never been here, though. Rigel 3 was a barren ball of rock and sand, a trading post and refuelling stop in a dreary sector of the galaxy. Kyle had wanted to go home – back to the colony on Altair 5 – as soon as they'd landed. So Dad had made him another promise. He'd said they'd spend as little time as possible on the planet, and that they could check out some sights on the way home – a spiral nebula or two, a gas cloud or a comet.

But Dad had broken that promise, too. They were just about to take off when he said he had a quick bit of business to sort out, and headed back into the port.

Kyle had kept busy by looking at his favourite website, space-exploration.com. He loved astronomy, and he was very interested in a little-known star system on the far side of the galaxy. It included a planet with some particularly fascinating features – a colossal range of volcanoes and a chain of islands made of some kind of seaweed.

But Dad had been gone for a couple of hours now, and Kyle was worried. He shouldn't have let Dad leave him behind. Gizmo was with him, of course, and he could put his pet into guard-dog mode at the press of a button. But that wasn't the point. He'd know what Dad was up to if he'd gone with him. Sometimes he had a habit of getting involved in what could only be described as "dodgy deals"...

Suddenly, Kyle heard the hatch door clang shut and footsteps hurrying through the ship. He looked round and saw Dad arriving on the bridge.

"OK, son?" Dad said.

Kyle noticed he was out of breath, as if he'd been running, and seemed a bit agitated.

Dad sat down and quickly began flipping switches on the main control panel. Screens and displays lit up, and Kyle felt the deck throb beneath his feet as the engines pulsed into life. "You'd better strap yourself in, Kyle. Liftoff in... 20 seconds."

"Well, no, actually I'm not OK, Dad..." muttered Kyle, struggling into his seat straps and trying to find Gizmo's, without success. This was typical of Dad, absolutely typical. One minute he's nowhere to be found, and the next he's in a tearing hurry to leave. "What took you so long?"

The ship's computer had begun an audio countdown. "*Ten… nine… eight… seven…*" the electronic voice was saying, quiet and calm.

"I don't have time to explain right now, Kyle," said Dad. He pressed another button. "Brace yourself. This is going to be rough."

"Hang on, Dad," said Kyle. "I haven't got Gizmo strapped in…"

It was too late. The engines roared and the *Happy Rakers* rose from the tarmac, then blasted high into the darkening sky. Kyle was pushed into his seat by the terrific G-force, his face distorted. He tried to hold on to Gizmo, but it was impossible. The little robodog flew over his shoulder and landed with a clang behind him.

Dad kept going at top speed as they left the atmosphere. They shot past Rigel 3's moon and the other planets in the system, several of which were enormous gas giants, and whizzed through a belt of ice-bound asteroids. He only slowed down when they entered deep space.

"Phew," said Dad, wiping his forehead. "Sorry about that, but we needed to get away from there pretty sharpish. Is Gizmo all right?"

"I think so," muttered Kyle, unstrapping himself and picking up the robodog, who nuzzled into his neck. "What's going on? Why did we need to lift off so quickly? Are you in trouble?"

"Trouble? Me?" said Dad, frowning. "Er... no, of course not. It's just that I knew you didn't like that place. Anyway, forget about that now, I've got some good news for you." He grinned. "I promised you a trip to World of Fun... and that's where we're going!"

"*WHAT*?" said Kyle, amazed. "But I thought we couldn't afford it."

"We can now," said Dad. He pulled a small disc from his pocket, slotted it into the computer and pressed DOWNLOAD. "At least we will once I've paid a visit to the co-ordinates on this disc. I'll take you home, go and do what I have to, then come back for you and Mum..."

Kyle was delighted by what he had just heard. But then he started feeling suspicious. "Hey, is this one of your dodgy deals?" he said. "I bet you've heard where you can get fake tickets for World of Fun, or maybe they're even stolen. Well, you can count me out. I'm too young to do time on the Prison Planet."

"I take great exception to your tone, Kyle," said Dad, giving him a wounded look. The big screen in front of them showed the stars rushing by. "I might *occasionally* bend the rules, but that's only because I'm trying to provide for my family. It's tough being a space trader."

"So is what you're doing legal?" said Kyle, arms folded.

"Er... I wouldn't go quite *that* far," said Dad, avoiding Kyle's gaze. "I mean part of it definitely is. I might even get a medal if I manage to pull it off. But part of it probably isn't. It will all be fine, though, I promise..."

Kyle was intrigued. How could it be

something that Dad might get a medal for *and* which might not be legal at the same time? He opened his mouth to reply – but there was a terrific *BANG*! and the *Happy Rakers* juddered from stern to tip. Another, even louder, *BANG*! followed, and another and, to his horror, Kyle realised they were being shot at!

"*Warning*!" said the computer. An alarm started to howl and red lights flashed across the screens. "*We are being attacked, repeat, attacked...*"

"Oh no, I don't believe it!" said Dad. "I was sure I'd fooled him!"

"Fooled who, Dad?" said Kyle, gripping the arms of his seat.

There was another huge *BANG*!

"I'll tell you later, once we've got away," said Dad. His fingers flashed over the control panel, and the *Happy Rakers* instantly began to pick up speed again. "Computer, boost power to the rear force field..."

"Don't worry," Kyle muttered. "I'll find out myself."

He turned to the panel beside the co-pilot's seat and punched in some instructions. Soon a small screen was giving him a view back towards the Rigel system. A large spaceship, bristling with laser weapons, was closing fast on them from behind. There was something familiar about it, too... Kyle scanned the image into the computer, looked it up – and then wished he hadn't.

"Er... Dad," he said, "did you know we're being chased by Tarkel the Vile, the most notorious pirate in the galaxy?"

"What?" said Dad, looking round, surprised. "Wow, you worked that out quickly. You're so clever, Kyle – your mum would be proud of you!" There was another *BANG!*, the loudest one so far, and the *Happy Rakers* rocked. "But actually, Tarkel is only number two in the pirate rankings. The number one villain is a charmer called Ogron the Unspeakable. Tarkel has been trying to knock

Ogron off the top spot for years."

"Oh, well, that's OK then," said Kyle. "He can't possibly do us any harm if he's only the *second* most notorious pirate in the galaxy."

"There's that tone of voice again," said Dad. "Sometimes you sound just like your mother."

"And I'm sure Mum would ask exactly the same question that I'm about to," said Kyle. "What have you done to upset Tarkel the Vile?"

"I sold him some spacesuits, that's all," said Dad. Kyle raised an eyebrow. "They were good as new, I swear. But he left me alone on the bridge of his ship for a while, so I took a quick peek at his computer databank. And I happened to find out something, er... very interesting."

"What was it?" said Kyle as they were rocked by another *BANG*!

"The co-ordinates of his hideout," said Dad. "The planet where he keeps his treasure. I mean, I knew I was taking a risk, but it was too good a chance to pass up. I can't understand how he found out so quickly."

"Did you close the page you'd been looking at?" said Kyle.

"Er..." Dad looked embarrassed. "Now you mention it, I don't think I did. I was in such a hurry to leave..."

"Well, there you go," said Kyle. "I should think the fact that we left the planet so quickly made him pretty suspicious, too. But what are you up to, Dad?" Kyle paused, and suddenly everything fell into place. "I know – your plan is to steal Tarkel's treasure, and only *then* hand over the planet's co-ordinates to the Space Police! That's how it can be legal *and* dodgy at the same time!"

"Spot on!" said Dad, grinning at his son again. "I know it's wrong, but I was only thinking about you and Mum. I'm fed up with struggling to make a living and I really want to take you to World of Fun. I'm pretty certain we can outrun Tarkel any day..."

"I wouldn't bet on it..." said Kyle,

glancing at his screen. Tarkel's ship almost filled it completely now and was getting closer by the second.

All of a sudden, there was a terrific *CRASH*! and it felt as if the *Happy Rakers* had come to a dead stop. Sparks fizzed from the control panel and the ship creaked ominously.

"*WARNING*!" said the computer, its voice not so calm any more. "*We have been seized in an energy beam and the hatch is being breached*!"

"Oh no, Tarkel must have docked with us!" said Dad, undoing his straps. He stood up, but it was too late to do anything.

Kyle heard a dull *BOOM*! as the hatch was blown in, followed by the clanging of heavy space boots on the decks. He unstrapped himself and stood beside his father, holding Gizmo.

"You'd better let me do the talking, son," said Dad, squeezing Kyle's shoulder.

"Somehow that doesn't make me feel any safer, Dad," Kyle muttered under his breath.

He loved his father, and he didn't blame him for what had happened. But he wasn't going to stand there while Dad made things worse, which usually happened when he did a lot of talking. No, Kyle had already come up with a plan – Plan A. He placed his finger on a large, red button at the back of Gizmo's neck, the one that put his pet in guard-dog mode. He just had to wait for the right moment...

Tarkel strode on to the bridge, six of his crew behind him. They were all pointing laser pistols at Kyle and his dad. So much for Plan A, thought Kyle, his heart sinking. Even Gizmo in guard-dog mode wouldn't be able to do anything against six laser pistols. It looked like he would have to move on to Plan B. It was a crazy idea, and very dangerous, but it might just work...

"Oh, hi there, Tarkel," said Dad with a big smile. "I'd have stopped if I'd realised it was you. Nothing wrong with those spacesuits, is there?"

"You know very well that's not why I'm here, Raker," said Tarkel. Kyle could see why the pirate was known as Tarkel the Vile. He certainly wouldn't have won any beauty competitions. He was a Reptilian, with scaly, green skin, a long tail and a mouth full of sharp teeth. His cold, yellow eyes were fixed menacingly on Kyle's father. "Give me one good reason why I shouldn't kill you and the brat right now," Tarkel hissed, raising his pistol.

"Er..." Dad said, a desperate look on his face. But Kyle spoke first.

"Because you'll miss out on the best chance you'll ever have of becoming the galaxy's Number One Villain," he said with a shrug.

"What are you talking about, boy?" growled Tarkel, turning to him.

"I told Dad we should never have tangled with you," said Kyle. "I knew you'd be too smart for us, and you were." Tarkel squared his shoulders and the six reptiles behind him nodded. "But I'm hoping you'll let us live if we delete the co-ordinates to your hideout from our computer," Kyle continued, "and give you the co-ordinates of someone else's instead. We can tell you where Ogron hides all his treasure..."

Tarkel was staring at Kyle with narrowed eyes, and for a moment Kyle thought that his bluff hadn't worked. Then Tarkel smiled – or at least Kyle assumed that's what he was doing with his mouth. It was hard to tell, but he had certainly opened it more widely.

"Explain yourself, boy," said Tarkel.

"There's not much to explain, really," said Kyle. "Dad came up with this plan to raid the hideouts of the top five pirates, and we paid a visit to Ogron first. You'll find what you need on my computer. It's the last planet I looked at, part of a little-known star system on the far side of the galaxy. But Ogron's not as sharp as you, Tarkel. He has no idea we know where his hideout is, so..."

"It will be a complete surprise when I, the great Tarkel the Vile, arrive," murmured the pirate, grinning even more. "Check what the boy says is true," he said. One of the others strode forward to access the computer. He searched for the last planet Kyle had looked at, found it, then turned and nodded to his leader. "Good," growled Tarkel. Download the co-ordinates and delete... everything else."

"Hey, you can't do that!" said Dad, suddenly finding his voice. "That computer contains a lot of valuable files!"

"I can do whatever I want, Raker," Tarkel hissed, whipping round to glare at Kyle's dad. "Just be grateful you're still alive. But I'm only granting you a temporary reprieve. I'm leaving one of my crew here on guard while I check these co-ordinates are accurate. And if they're not, I'll make you suffer – got it?"

Tarkel didn't wait for Dad to reply. He strode off the bridge with five of his crew. A few moments later, Kyle heard Tarkel's ship undock and the *Happy Rakers'* hatch being quickly resealed by the emergency repair systems.

The pirate who had checked the computer stayed behind, keeping watch on Dad and Kyle, his laser pistol pointed at them.

"Nice try, son," Dad whispered at last. "But what do we do now?"

"*We're* not going to do anything," Kyle whispered back. He was still holding Gizmo, and he still had his finger on the red button. "Gizmo is..."

Kyle pressed the red button and dropped his pet. Gizmo landed on his feet and instantly began to grow, his legs shooting up, his head and body doubling, then trebling in size. The pirate aimed his pistol at the robodog, but he was too late. Gizmo easily batted the weapon out of the reptile's paw then *ROARED* at him. The pirate screamed in terror and fled into the depths of the ship, with Gizmo in hot pursuit.

"Wow, I never realised just how good the guard-dog mode is," said Kyle, shaking his head. "I don't think that guy is going to give us any more bother. And now I suggest we set a course for the nearest Space Police station and give them the co-ordinates to Tarkel's hideout…"

"But we don't have them," said Dad. "He deleted our files."

"No, he didn't, Dad," said Kyle with a sigh. "The computer's got a back-up facility, remember? I put it in for you last year."

"Oh, right," said Dad, and smiled. "Hey, maybe there's a reward for information about Tarkel – enough for three tickets to World of Fun." His smile vanished. "But if there is, I'll have to explain all this to your mum. You will help me come up with a good story, won't you?"

"Sure, Dad, absolutely *no* problem," said Kyle, taking his seat again and punching a new course into the control panel. "That's a promise."

EVERYTHING
I NEED

It was a bright, autumn day in London, and a boy was picking his way round the remains of the great fallen column in Trafalgar Square. He was about 12, with dark hair, wearing a hooded jacket, combat trousers and heavy boots. The boy stopped by a rusty, bombed-out tank to get his bearings, shielding his eyes from the morning sun and easing the straps of his backpack. He had visited most parts of the ruined city during the last few months, but not this one, and he didn't want to get lost.

There was a strangely familiar quality about the place, though. A memory was trying to push itself up from the depths of his mind, a sunny image from before The Bad Time – voices, laughter, something sweet and cold on his tongue...

The boy scowled, got himself under control and forced the image down, then turned to look behind him. He gave a low whistle. A big dog, its black coat covered in dust, scrabbled over a heap of rubble and trotted up beside him, pushing its nose into his hand.

"What have you been doing, Alfie, you naughty dog?" said the boy, roughly brushing the dust off. He was smiling as he said it, and the dog stood still to be cleaned, obedient and trusting. But suddenly Alfie growled softly, and the boy felt him stiffen under his hands.

"Hello," said a quiet voice, the sound echoing eerily off the ruins. "That's a nice dog you've got there. He won't bite me though, will he?"

The boy whirled round, whipping a knife from his belt and holding it out in front of him, ready to fight, every muscle tensed.

The voice belonged to a girl his age. She was standing a few metres away, and he guessed she must have come out of one of the buildings on the street beyond the square. Several seemed more or less intact, although they were all pockmarked with bullet holes. The fighting here must have been pretty fierce.

"He will if I tell him to," said the boy, and started to back off. "So don't come any closer."

The girl didn't look very dangerous. She was smaller than him, and skinny in her old parka, jeans and trainers, her fair hair hanging to her shoulders, her green eyes focused on his blade. But he'd learned long ago you could never tell what a person was like from the way they looked. She might be mad, or infected with something deadly.

"Don't worry, I haven't got a disease or anything," the girl said quickly, as if she could read his mind. "And I don't want to hurt you. It would just be nice to talk to someone. You're the first person I've seen for ages."

"Think yourself lucky, then," muttered the boy with a shrug. "People are usually just bad news." He turned to walk away. "Come on, Alfie."

"Please don't go!" the girl said quickly. "I've got food I can give you, and I could probably find some for your dog, too. You'd like something nice to eat, wouldn't you, Alfie?" She was speaking directly to Alfie, smiling at him.

To the boy's surprise, the dog stopped growling. His ears pricked up, and he wagged his tail. Usually Alfie was as suspicious of strangers as his master, and made sure they kept away. But he seemed to have taken an instant liking to this girl.

"There you are," she said, grinning now. "Alfie thinks you should stay."

The boy turned back and looked her up and down. "I don't see any food," he said warily. The girl wasn't carrying a bag or a backpack, and his practised eyes told him that her pockets were empty. "So where is it?"

"Not far, in one of those buildings," she said, pointing with her thumb over her shoulder. "I've been living there for the last couple of weeks."

The boy stared at her. He was irritated by the way she'd used Alfie's name so freely. Going with her would break the rule he had made for himself, too, and that he was trying hard to keep – he had sworn to steer clear of people, to have absolutely nothing to do with them. But the girl was holding his gaze, looking at him with those wide, green eyes of hers, waiting for his answer. Alfie obviously didn't think she was a threat, and the offer of food was very tempting. Pickings were getting pretty scarce these days, especially south of the river where he'd been holed up for a while. Searching for food was the reason he had come here, after all.

"OK," the boy said at last.

The girl smiled and strode off, and Alfie was soon trotting along beside her, his tail wagging even more. The boy followed them. He realised he was still holding his knife, and he slipped it back in the sheath, although he kept his hand on the hilt. His eyes flicked constantly from side to side, his senses alert for any danger. He would eat the food the girl was offering and be on his way, he told himself, make it back to his own place long before the sun had gone down. In most parts of the city it still wasn't a good idea to be on the streets after dark.

"Here we are," said the girl at last, stopping outside a building. It had been a huge bookshop once, but its windows were smashed and the books lay ripped and torn and scattered across the floor, filthy with dust and bloated from the rain that had blown in over the years. The girl glanced shyly at the boy. "Well, not *exactly* here," she said, flicking her hair back behind her ears. "It's a lot cleaner and nicer downstairs, honest."

She walked to the back of the shop and picked up a torch from a shelf. There was a click, and a beam of light shot out, illuminating a curving staircase that descended into deep darkness. "This way," said the girl, and went down, Alfie running after her without a backward glance. The boy hesitated briefly, and then followed them, the torchlight a moving beacon ahead of him, the rubble dust on the stairs crunching under his soles.

Soon he found himself in a large basement that wasn't as badly damaged as the upstairs part of the shop. At any rate, most of the walls were still lined with books, as far as the boy could tell. The girl finally stopped, took a lamp from another shelf and switched it on.

The boy saw they were in the children's books section of the shop, the soft, yellow lamplight gleaming on colourful covers and spines. It was almost perfectly preserved, a little oasis from the old days. The kind of place the boy usually avoided like the plague.

A door in one wall led to a small office, where the girl had made her camp. Its original occupant was long gone, almost certainly dead, and the girl had pushed back the desk with its useless computer to make room for her sleeping bag and a portable cooker fuelled by a gas cylinder. The boy's eyes quickly took in what else she had – a stock of canned food, a variety of bottles filled with water, a rucksack stuffed with clothes. But he also noticed a worn teddy bear tucked in the top of the sleeping bag, the corners of some photographs poking up beside it. A paperback lay beside the sleeping bag, a bookmark in its pages.

"It's not much, but I call it home," said the girl. She sat on the floor and smiled up at him. "At least, for the time being. Anyway, don't just stand there, make yourself comfortable. We should introduce ourselves. I know already this is Alfie..." She paused to fondle the dog's big, floppy ears, and Alfie rolled his eyes with pleasure. "My name's Eve. What's yours?"

The boy had been standing in the doorway. Now he entered and took off his backpack, dumping it in a corner as far from the girl as possible. He sat down beside it, one arm over its top, his legs crossed. He clicked his fingers, summoning Alfie to his side. The dog reluctantly obeyed.

"What about that food, then?" the boy said, refusing to answer the girl's question and avoiding her eager gaze. He wouldn't be staying long, so there was no need to get all chummy with her now, was there?

"Coming right up," said the girl, her smile faltering slightly. But she turned her attention to the cooker, and soon recovered her poise. "You're not much of a talker, are you?" she added, not looking at him. "Oh well, I don't mind. I'll tell you about myself first, then maybe you can join in..."

But the boy stayed grimly silent as the girl talked and talked. Her story was one that held no surprises for him. Life in a nice house with her parents and two older brothers, and a couple of dogs. School with lots of friends, and holidays and sleepovers, and presents at Christmas and birthdays. Everything safe and secure, or so they all thought.

Then the war came, and cities were wrecked and millions died, and most of those who didn't went mad and killed each other or caught diseases and died anyway. Eve didn't say what had happened to her family. Just that she had been on her own for ages, and had learned how to stay alive.

The boy sat watching her stir the contents of a tin of meat stew in a saucepan over the cooker's blue flame, until her voice faded away and his own memories took over. At least, the few memories he allowed himself to examine from time to time, the bare, brutal outlines of what he had suffered. His own parents and little sister had been killed by looters, and he had only survived because he'd hidden in a cupboard. Another family had taken him in for a while, but they had died from disease, and after that he had started to stay away from people. After all, it was people who had started the war, and the survivors were a total waste of time. Either they wanted to do bad things to you, or they were nice – and died. It was better to be alone and take care of yourself, and not think about the past. He had got into the habit of forcing down any nice memories that tried to surface. Although sometimes that was hard. Very hard.

"Right, there you go," the girl said at last, handing the boy his plate of steaming meat stew and a spoon. "And here's yours, Alfie. You've been so patient."

The dog gave a little whine of pleasure as Eve put a bowl of meat in front of him, and he quickly began to gobble it down. The boy ate slowly, enjoying every rich mouthful.

"So what about you?" Eve said quietly, after a while. She hadn't touched her food. "What's your story?"

"I don't have one," the boy muttered, hunching over his plate.

"You must have," said Eve, smiling at him again. "Didn't you have a family before... before The Bad Time?" She put down her plate and pulled the photographs from her sleeping bag. "This is mine," she said. "My mum and dad and my brothers, and these are our dogs, Billy and Ben. Don't you think Billy is the spitting image of your Alfie? I do..."

The boy stared at the happy faces in the photographs. The girl was right, one of the dogs in the pictures *did* look like Alfie. And there was something else. Another of the photographs had been taken in Trafalgar Square, when the column had still been standing and families had come here on days out, to mingle with the tourists and have fun.

The boy took the photograph and held it, studying it – the smiling parents and children, Eve in the middle, crowds behind them. And slowly the memory that had tried to surface when he had arrived in the square began to force its way into his mind. Just like Eve, he too had been to Trafalgar Square on an outing with his family long ago.

Suddenly a dam seemed to burst in his mind and it all came flooding back; images and sounds and feelings from that day filling his head however hard he tried to push them down and deny them. Sitting on his dad's shoulders, his mum and sister laughing, the smell of the pizza and the taste of the ice cream they'd eaten later. Yes, ice cream, that was what had been so cold and oh so sweet. His mouth started to water, and other memories followed, more images of his mum and dad and his lovely little green-eyed sister. Now he felt his eyes filling with hot tears, his throat closing, his heart pounding wildly in his chest...

"It's a nice picture, isn't it?" the girl said wistfully. "That's why I came here to live for a while. "This place brings back some good memories."

The boy closed his eyes and concentrated hard, struggling to get himself under control, stop these thoughts, make sure he didn't cry.

"Not for me, it doesn't," he said at last, opening his eyes. He threw the photograph at the girl and jumped to his feet, the plate and spoon falling from his lap to the floor with a clatter.

The girl scrabbled away and looked at him, alarmed.

"Come on, Alfie," the boy snapped, grabbing the dog's collar with one hand, picking up his backpack with the other and swinging it over his shoulder. "It's time we left. Thanks for the food."

"Wait, don't go," the girl pleaded. She stood up quickly and came towards him, reaching out a hand. "We should stick together, you and me. You're just as lonely as I am. I knew it the moment I first saw you."

"You're wrong," said the boy, pausing in the doorway. "I don't want to get tied up with anyone, it just doesn't work. I've got everything I need."

"I don't believe you," said the girl. "And neither does Alfie."

The dog was standing between them, whining softly, his ears and tail drooping. He looked at the boy, then at the girl, and back at the boy again.

"You can believe what you like," said the boy. "But we're going."

He turned away from her, from her outstretched hand, and hurried towards the staircase. He stomped up the gritty stairs and strode through the shop, kicking bloated books out of his way, listening for the sound of paws scrabbling behind him and not hearing it. He stopped by the shop doorway and whistled. Alfie finally shot up the stairs and ran over to him, his ears pressed flat against his head. The boy carried on, marching back into the square, eventually coming to a halt by the bombed-out tank.

He was breathing hard, his hands were shaking, he was still having to hold back the flood of memories the girl's photo had unleashed. She had turned out to be dangerous after all, although not in a way he could have possibly imagined. Who did she think she was, infecting him with her madness, her talk of the past? Maybe she could deal with it, but he couldn't. If he really let himself remember what he'd lost, he wouldn't be able to live a single day more in this awful, solitary, *lonely* present.

There was that word the girl had used, the boy realised, and he sighed, his shoulders suddenly sagging. She was right, he *was* lonely, even if he had been determined not to admit it to himself. Sometimes he was so lonely he didn't think he could carry on. If the truth were known, he had been looking for more than food on his trips round ruined London. Like the girl, he had been looking for someone to talk to, another human being to be with when the night came and darkness filled the world.

But he was afraid, so afraid of what might happen if he found that person. What if he did stay with Eve and they became friends, but then she got ill and died? What if they met bad people who killed her? What if she turned out to be mad or horrible in some way after all? He couldn't stand it if he allowed himself to hope again and he just got hurt.

The boy shivered, and looked up to see that the sun had gone behind a bank of dark-grey clouds. A chill wind swirled the dust round his boots, and he had a vision of himself walking down endless, empty streets for the rest of his life, the ruined houses on either side full of ghosts whispering his name, begging him to come and join them.

Beside him, Alfie whined softly and nudged his leg, reminding his master that he was still there. The boy looked down at him and smiled.

"You like her, don't you?" he said, rubbing the dog's head. "And you don't care about the rest. It doesn't even occur to you."

The boy looked round at the bookshop with its smashed windows. Eve hadn't followed them out, and he wondered what she was doing down there in her basement, what she was thinking. Just then the sun slipped from behind the clouds, but it was low in a pink-streaked sky, and the boy realised it was getting late. He knew he really ought to leave now if he was going to make it back across the river to his place before sunset.

He stood for a moment longer – then walked towards the bookshop. Alfie ran along beside him, obviously not quite able to believe his luck at first, and then bounded off ahead when they reached the top of the stairs. He vanished into the dark, and the boy followed him, his shoes crunching on the gritty steps once more.

Eve was kneeling on her sleeping bag hugging Alfie when the boy found her. Alfie was licking her face and whining with pleasure. She looked up and saw the boy, the yellow lamplight reflected in her eyes.

"Is there any more of that stew?" he said. "It was pretty good."

"Maybe," said Eve, shrugging and pushing Alfie down. "But I'll only give it to you on one condition. You have to tell me your name, OK?"

"My name is… Adam," said the boy. It had been a long time since he had spoken his name aloud, but oddly enough it still sounded the same.

"Nice to meet you, Adam," said Eve. "I'm glad you came back."

Outside, the empty streets waited for the future to begin.

ABOUT THE AUTHOR

Tony Bradman was born and still lives in London. He has written a large number of books for children of all ages, including 25 titles about his most popular creation, Dilly the Dinosaur. *Dilly the Dinosaur* was made into a long-running TV series and one of the books was shortlisted for the Children's Book Award. Tony has also edited many anthologies of poetry and short stories.

Tony has always loved science fiction, and read enormous amounts of it when he was young. His favourite sci-fi authors are H.G. Wells, who wrote *The Time Machine* and *War of the Worlds*, and John Wyndham, who wrote *Day of the Triffids*. Tony also loves sci-fi movies, and has watched some of his favourites literally dozens of times!

Titles available for Year 6

Comparing Work of Significant Authors: Short Stories

Shock Forest and Other Stories • Margaret Mahy

Sky Ship and Other Stories • Geraldine McCaughrean

Snow Horse and Other Stories • Joan Aiken

Shakespeare Retellings

Macbeth • Tony Bradman

Romeo and Juliet • Michael Cox

The Tempest • Franzeska G. Ewart

Comparing Fiction Genres

Shadow Puppet and other ghost stories • Jane Clarke

Space Pirates and other sci-fi stories • Tony Bradman

Dark Eagle and other historical stories • Neil Tonge